P9-CRE-251

RAH, RAH, radishes

A VEGETABLE CHANT

by april pulley sayre

Beach Lane Books
New York London Toronto Sydney

For Isabel Baker of the Book Vine for Children
and Jack and Elaine of Hovenkamp's Produce—we did it!

Thank you to the farmers of the South Bend Farmers' Market for growing food to nourish our family and for allowing me to photograph your artistic vegetable displays. Additional thanks to Vaughn, Carol, and all the folks at Wolf Farms Perennials and More. Mary K, your peppers sing. Thank you, Jeff, for believing, brainstorming, and laying out the first prototype. Gratitude to reviewers Dr. George Knowles, Dr. Candace Corson, and Bethany Thayer, MS, RD, Center for Health Promotion and Disease Prevention. Candace, a huge hug for cheering on this project year after year. (Barb, you too!) This little book is a salute to my farming family, whose roots reach back generations in the Mississippi, Virginia, and South Carolina soils. I am especially remembering Granville Hough, who taught so many about the land.

BEACH LANE BOOKS • An imprint of Simon & Schuster Children's Publishing Division • 1230 Avenue of the Americas, New York, New York 10020 • Book design by Lauren Rille and Karina Granda • The text for this book is set in Calvert.• Manufactured in China • 0311 SCP • First Edition • 10 9 8 7 6 5 4 3 2 1 • Library of Congress Cataloging-in-Publication Data • Sayre, April Pulley. • Rah, rah, radishes! : a vegetable chant/April Pulley Sayre.—1st ed. • p. cm. • ISBN 978-1-4424-2141-7 (hardcover) • 1. Radishes—Juvenile literature. 2. Children's poetry. I. Title. • SB351.R3S39 2011 • 641.3'5—dc22 • 2010034360

Rah, rah, radishes!

Red and white.

Carrots are calling.
Take a bite!

Oh boy, bok choy!

Brussels sprout.

Broccoli. Cauliflower.
Shout it out!

Pile up peppers—
bananas, bells.

Crunch their colors.
Smell their smells!

Call for cayenne.
Pick poblano.

Hola, habanero!
Jalapeño, serrano!

Lettuce. Lima.

Go, green bean!

Cucumber's cool.
Kohlrabi's queen!

Eggplant's extraordinary.
Pumpkin's art.

Don't eat zucchini?
Time to start!

Snag some sweet corn!
Shuck an ear.

Celebrate celery.

Give a cheer!

Onion. Scallion.
Leek and shallot.

Grab that garlic.
Please your palate!

Head for cabbage.
Greens for sale.

Fall for fennel, Swiss chard, kale!

Root for rutabagas.
Bounce for beets!

Pile up parsnips.
Turnip treats!

Stash some squash. Fill your cupboard!

**Butternut, buttercup,
acorn, Hubbard!**

Potatoes. Tomatoes.
Yum a yam!

Slice 'em. Mash 'em.

Wham! Wham! Wham!

Ask for asparagus.
Pea pods, please.

Thank you, farmers.
Thank you, bees.

Sun and seasons, leaf and stalk.

Know them. Grow them!

Veggies

Cherry
Tomato
2.00
Box
3/5.00
2.00
Box
3/5.00
BELL
PEPPER
2/1.00
GARL
2/1.0

rock!

A Few More Bites

What is a vegetable?

A vegetable is any edible part of a plant that is not a nut or a sweet fruit. The word "vegetable" is a casual term, not a scientific one. This causes some confusion. To a scientist, the word "fruit" means "a plant's seed-bearing structure." By this definition, vegetables such as eggplants, cucumbers, and pumpkins are fruit. However, in everyday language, most people use the word "fruit" only for *sweet* seed-bearing structures, such as berries, apples, and peaches. The rest are called vegetables.

What about tomatoes? In 1893, the U.S. Supreme Court declared the tomato a vegetable—for tax purposes. Because imported vegetables were taxed and imported fruits were not, this declaration allowed taxes to be collected on imported tomatoes. Ask any scientist and they will tell you a tomato is still, despite the court case, technically a fruit.

Be the Baron of Broccoli! The Colonel of Corn! The Cauliflower Queen!

Young or old, you can become a vegetable expert for your family. Pick a vegetable. Read about it. Ask cooks, grocers, and farmers about it. Learn how to choose it, clean it, and cook it. Gather new recipes. Then when you have learned that vegetable, move on to another.

Color Your Plate

A healthy diet has lots of different natural colors. Natural colors are grown by nature, not by adding coloring when cooking or packaging food.

When you put together a plate of food, try to make it as full of different natural colors as possible. Go for green, yellow, orange, red, purple, and blue. Add some onions or garlic for white, too.

Veggies That Didn't Make the Cut

Fans of rhubarb, taro, collard greens, and other vegetables missing from this book, please don't get steamed. You can find these and other vegetables, vegetable facts, and yummy photos at AprilSayre.com.

Note: No vegetables were harmed or mistreated in the making of this book. Most, however, were later eaten.

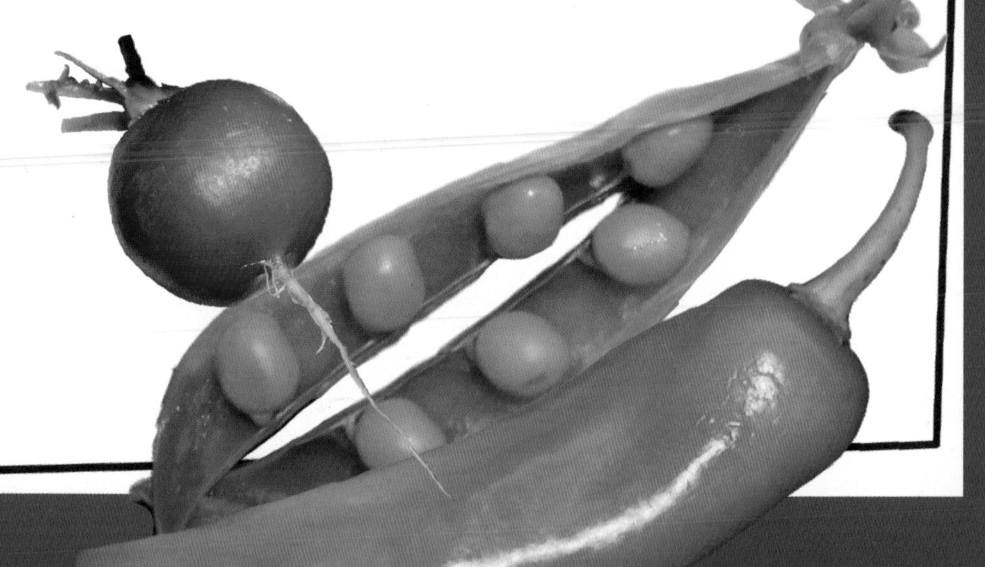